Hell-ectric Guitar

Hell-ectric Guitar

Brian McGinn

Nelson

an International Thomson Publishing company I(T)P®

Melbourne • Albany, NY • Belmont, CA • Bonn • Boston • Cincinnati
Detroit • Johannesburg • London • Madrid • Mexico City • New York
Paris • Singapore • Tokyo • Toronto • Washington

Nelson I(T)P®
102 Dodds Street
South Melbourne 3205

Email nelsonitp@nelson.com.au
Website http://www.nelsonitp.com

Nelson I(T)P® *an International Thomson Publishing company*

First published in 1998
10 9 8 7 6 5 4
05 04 03 02 01 00 99

Copyright © Nelson ITP 1999

National Library of Australia
Cataloguing-in-Publication data

Brian McGinn
    Hell-electric Guitar
    ISBN 0 17 009435 9
    ISBN 0 17 009414 6 (set).
    I. Title. (Series: BlitzIt).
    A823.3

Editorial production by BDP
Designed by Christine Deering
Illustrations by Grant Adam/Uncommon Characters
Cover designed by Grant Adam/Uncommon Characters
Text designed by Christine Deering
Typeset in Clearface Regular
Printed in Singapore by Kin Keong Printing Co. Pte. Ltd

Nelson Australia Pty Limited ACN 058 280 149 (incorporated in
Victoria) trading as Nelson ITP.

Contents

Chapter 1

Signed in Blood

Frank gazed through the window of the creepy looking shop. He wanted to buy a guitar, and a kid at school had suggested that the shop was worth checking out. The old guy who owned it was a bit strange, but anything you wanted, he had it.

Frank hesitated. The shop didn't look like the sort of place that would sell electric guitars. In fact, the window was so dirty and cobwebby Frank couldn't see anything at all.

"What's the point?" he murmured to himself. "I might as well give up."

Suddenly, from out of nowhere, a large dark cloud appeared and rained right on him. Frank pushed the door open and ran into the shop. It was so dark that he couldn't see a thing. Even worse, it smelt off, like a bag of dirty socks on a hot day. Frank felt his way to the counter and hit the skull bell.

"Hey! Anyone around?" There was silence.

Behind the counter was a large collection of bottles arranged on a sagging shelf. Inside the bottles, floating in greenish liquid, were all sorts of weird things: bugs; spiders; false teeth; a vampire bat.

"What *is* this shop?" Frank stumbled around. In one corner was a mummy's coffin. Against the back wall stood a row of tombstones. But no electric guitars.

Frank had turned to walk out when an enormous black cupboard became visible in the shadows. A cold shiver curled his toes, went up his spine and out through his hair. It was as if a voice in his head was telling him that what he wanted was in the cupboard. Frank tried the door but the cupboard was locked. The handle felt strange, as if it was electrified.

"Have to open cupboard." Frank drooled; his eyes pulsated. He pulled again at the handle but it wouldn't budge.

"Have to open cupboard!" He spat on his hands then grabbed the handle firmly. Placing his left foot against the cupboard, he pulled with all his weight.

CRASH! With a splintering of wood the door fell open. Frank flew across the room and ricocheted off the far wall. Dense black smoke filled the shop. Frank heard the sound of a dog howling at the moon. But, slowly, he crawled back to the cupboard.

3

Inside was a guitar case. A battered, black electric-guitar case. Frank's mouth was as dry as a dead rat's tail. He pulled at the lock on the case; it was shut tight. He moaned.

"What are you doing there, boy?" a voice a thousand-years-old spat at Frank. A downright ugly old dude glared down at him with yellow, cat-like eyes. A putrid odour wafted from his filthy clothes. Sulphur?

Frank backed away from him. "I just wanted to look at the guitar."

"You want to look at the guitar, hey?"

Frank nodded, his head going a hundred beats to the second.

The old man pulled out a long, silver dagger from his pocket. Frank wanted to run but was welded to the spot.

The old man sniggered. The knife flashed, then turned into a key which he jiggled in the lock on the case. The case flew open, and there lay a guitar. And not just any guitar – a

Stratocaster. It was old, burnt up and twisted; in bad need of new machine heads and pickups. The vibrato bar had lost all its shine and was crusted with rust. The fretboard was pitted and scratched. The strings were green with disuse. But Frank wanted it more than he'd wanted *anything* in his life.

"Can I pick it up?"

The old man licked his lips. His voice was like gravel in a cage. "If the guitar lets you."

Frank strapped on the guitar. He felt it wrap itself around him, like a snake.

"It likes you. Would you like to play it?"

"I can't. I only know how to play an acoustic."

The old man shuffled out to a back room and came back with a hundred-watt Marshall amp from the back of the shop. He plugged the instrument in. "The guitar will tell you what to do. Play."

Frank placed his fingers on the strings and

felt a tingle go through them, like he'd dipped his hand in lukewarm water. The feeling surged through his entire body.

He pulled his favourite pick out of his pocket and started to play. Well, really well. Piping hot, in fact. He played guitar licks he didn't know; played so fast he couldn't see his fingers moving. He sounded exactly like a big-time rock guitarist. A wail of feedback filled the room, and Frank stopped playing and fell to his knees. He was gasping.

"How much?"

The old man smirked. "You don't have enough for this instrument."

"I have to have it. I'll give you anything for it."

"Anything?"

"Anything."

"Just a drop of blood will do."

Frank stuck out an index finger.

The old man pulled a dusty, yellow piece of paper from a pocket. The key in his hand flashed and, suddenly, became a long pin. "Just bleed here. At the bottom of the page. It's a contract between us."

Frank hesitated. "I don't know..."

"I'll throw in the amplifier."

The blood dripped easily from Frank's finger.

Chapter 2

Red Hot

Frank's mum gazed at the guitar. She thought he'd been ripped off.

"Take a look at it. It's old and burnt."

"It doesn't matter what it looks like, Mum. It's what it *sounds* like that counts. A real guitar is something you make music with. It's not a fashion accessory. Appearance doesn't mean anything."

From the moment Frank had strapped on the guitar, he felt different. Stronger. Smarter.

He even spoke differently now. "You don't wear a guitar. You play it."

"But you can't play an electric guitar, can you, Frank?" asked his mum.

"Is that so? Get a load of this."

Frank sat his mother down at the kitchen table, strapped on the guitar and turned on the amp. He placed his fingers on the strings and immediately felt that tingling warmth all over. The old man in the shop had told him to clear his mind, then imagine. The guitar would do the rest.

Frank imagined he was on his surfboard, right out the back of the waves. It was a perfect swell. He could feel the saltwater splashing on him; the wind blowing up the beach; the sheer exhilaration of catching the perfect wave.

It all came out through the guitar.

When he finished playing his mother's mouth hung wide open.

"Read them and weep." Frank took a bow.

"What an unbelievable sound. I can't

explain it, but the music reminded me of the beach. And my darling boy played it!" His mother squeezed him tightly.

Frank smiled to himself. Of course he had played it. The guitar just brought out his natural talent, by helping him to move his fingers to the right places at the right times. But at the heart of it was *his* playing.

"But you will at least paint it, won't you?" asked his mother.

• • •

Frank did try to paint the guitar, but as soon as he brought the paint brush near it his hand quivered and ached. So he dropped that idea. Another idea he'd come up with was much better, and the guitar seemed to agree with this one. Frank was going to join a band.

• • •

The Cool Cucumbers rehearsed in Crunchy's garage. Frank could hear the music from the street. Well, it wasn't actually music as such.

More like a bunch of guys playing off-key and out-of-tempo. A bunch of bad notes thrown together. The band was awful.

Frank knocked hard on the door. The noise came to an off-key halt and Crunchy yelled: "This had better be important! We're rehearsing, you know." He threw open the door.

Frank smiled at him. "Is that what you call it?"

"What do you want, nerd?"

"I've come to join your band."

"Yeah, right. What are you going to play? The fool?" Crunchy and the other band members – Bongo on drums and Duck on bass – laughed like drains.

"I'm your new lead guitarist."

"What are you talking about, birdbrain? *I'm* the lead guitarist."

"Just let me try out. If you play better than I do, then I'll lick your shoes for a whole year."

"You're on."

Frank set up his amp and strapped on his guitar.

"What do you call that?" Crunchy looked at Frank's guitar.

"Just shut up and play. I'll do the rest. Give me a blues riff."

Frank didn't know half the stuff he was talking about. He didn't know a blues riff from a blue rinse, but what the heck. He placed his fingers on the strings, and he and the guitar connected. He counted the band in.

One, two, three, four.

The band played the riff. Frank imagined a racing car going through the corners at two hundred kilometres-an-hour; tyres squealing and rubber burning; the car going through a blanket of red-hot fire.

Frank and the guitar joined in. The guitar's sound was loud, abrasive and raw, like a fresh piece of meat.

Frank played sextuplets, septuplets, grupettos

and half-notes, then went down to duplets and triples, and back up to cosmic notes. He kept perfect time with the band throughout.

The Cool Cucumbers had never played better. It was as if the magic of Frank's playing had taken possession of them all. Frank finished on the twenty-third fret; a high, ear-piercing note.

He gazed at three opened-mouthed faces. "So am I in?"

"For sure," said Bongo.

"For *sure!*" said Duck.

"Now hang on. I'm lead guitarist." Crunchy looked a bit peeved.

"*He's* a lead guitarist. You're a ..." Bongo blurted it out before he knew what he was saying.

Frank knew that it was Crunchy's garage, and that the band would need somewhere to practise. "You're right. You *are* the lead guitarist."

"But you play rings around me."

Frank acted like he was thinking. "Hang on, I've got it. Why don't you be the lead singer and rhythm guitarist?"

"Lead singer and rhythm guitarist?"

"Girls love lead singers," Frank added.

"Yeah?" Crunchy smiled to himself.

So that's how Frank joined the band.

• • •

When Frank arrived home he was so hungry that he ate, and ate, and ate. Playing the guitar seemed to drain him. Then, suddenly, he felt incredibly tired and crashed into bed. Only then did he notice how much his hands hurt, like he'd walked a hundred kilometres on them.

Chapter 3

First Gig

Over the next few weeks the band rehearsed. Frank did some mind-boggling things on the guitar. When he played he felt like he was king of the world. Then he'd go home, eat like a horse, then collapse into bed with aching hands. His life revolved around eating, sleeping and playing his guitar. He was the happiest he'd ever been in his life.

• • •

The band's first gig was at the local Blue Light Disco. Crunchy had organised it. He knew the Sergeant who ran the Police Boys' Club. All the kids from school, their parents, relatives… everyone was there.

Frank's feet hurt. His knees quivered. His stomach churned. His heart was racing at five thousand kilometres-an-hour. He had the worst headache of his life. Worst of all, his hands were as stiff as boards. How was he going to play guitar? He hoped the guitar wouldn't let him down.

Crunchy noticed Frank's nervousness. "Ready for this?"

"I want to go to the toilet again." Frank winced in pain.

"No, come on, let's get on with it." Crunchy was so cool about performing it was as if he was born for it.

The Cool Cucumbers took to the stage. Most of the crowd cheered and one or two heckled.

Frank's dad was wearing a terrible tie-dyed shirt and bell-bottom pants. He thought he looked mega-cool. He'd been up dancing even before the music started. What a goose. Dad had played in a band many years ago. He still had his old amp in the garage.

Crunchy yelled into the mike, "We're the Cool Cucumbers. Are you ready to rock?!"

Everyone, especially Frank's dad, yelled and clapped loudly. Crunchy counted in the tempo and the band – except Frank – started playing.

Frank's hands hung by his side. He looked at the crowd, and at his dad and mum. He wanted to vomit. He wanted to run away and never be seen again. What was he thinking of? What was he doing up on stage?

Then he placed his fingers on the strings of the guitar. The guitar's warmth entered his body. Suddenly, he knew he was going to be okay. He cleared his mind, thought of flying through the sky – and started playing.

● ● ●

17

The band members' parents were astounded with how good the band was, especially Frank. They said he was an absolute genius on the guitar. Frank's dad had a big stupid grin from ear to ear. Frank had never seen him pump his chest out so much. "A chip off the old block," Dad said. "It's obvious."

"As long as he's happy, I'm happy." Frank's mum gently ruffled his hair. She forced a smile.

The Sergeant came over and shook Frank's hand. "Son, that was some of the best guitar playing I've heard in a long time. In fact, the last time I heard guitar playing like that was by Jimi Hendrix, way back in the sixties. I've booked you and the Cool Cucumbers for the next six discos."

Frank and the band had arrived.

• • •

That night, as Frank lay in bed, he thought about the performance. His hands, arms and shoulders ached, but he didn't care. Finding that guitar had been the best thing that had ever happened to him. He smiled at how proud his mum and dad were of him. He never wanted the feeling to end.

Suddenly, the sheets felt damp. Frank pulled his hand out from under the doona, and what he saw made him feel faint. The pin-prick the old man had given him was oozing fresh, red blood. His hand was covered in it.

The room started spinning round, and round, and round. Frank's ears were ringing. He felt incredibly cold and his teeth started to chatter. His body felt so light that it started to lift off the bed. Frank could see a bright light racing towards him. Then suddenly, it all stopped. He gasped and everything went black.

The next morning, when he woke up, Frank decided it had just been a bad dream.

Chapter 4

Shocking!

Over the next few weeks the Cool Cucumbers attracted a solid following at the disco. A guy from the local newspaper came to interview the band. Or, more to the point, Frank.

"So how long have you been playing?" the reporter asked.

"Only a few weeks," Frank answered.

"And you're this good?"

"I play from the soul, man." Frank was coming out with a few cool lines.

"Yeah, right. Do you mind if I have a look at your guitar?"

Frank smiled. "No, be my guest."

The journalist strummed the guitar. "It's pretty battered, but it sure produces some beautiful sounds."

Frank was cocky. "It all depends on who's playing it."

The journalist left without interviewing the rest of the band. Crunchy and the others looked pretty mad. "Hey, didn't he want to talk to us?" grouched Crunchy.

Frank wasn't listening. "He thinks I'm not playing the guitar. He thinks there's a tape somewhere; that I'm faking it."

"But what about the band?" Crunchy yelled out the window at the journalist, who was halfway down the street.

Frank gritted his teeth "Well, it *is* me playing it. No-one can prove otherwise."

• • •

A month later Frank sat watching himself on television and felt great. Really great. All tingly. The Cool Cucumbers were in the background, but most of the footage was of Frank, and of course he came up well. Dad had designed his outfit – leather pants and a purple jacket. The television reporter called Frank a genius. There was that word again. Frank liked hearing it said in the same breath as his name.

Could one boy's life be any better? People had started noticing him. He'd become the number-one kid at school; he even had his own fan club. Girls swooned at his feet. Boys stepped aside when he walked by.

A couple of guys had tried to give him a hard time, but soon after were involved in strange accidents. One fell from a ladder and broke his arm; another was stung by a hive of bees.

Frank sat strumming his guitar on screen. The reporter asked Frank whether he wanted to be the next Nathan Cavaleri.

"I can play rings around him," Frank smugly replied.

A few short weeks ago he'd just been a nerd. Now he was on his way to becoming a national celebrity. Finding that guitar *was* the best thing that had ever happened to him. What luck!

• • •

At the next rehearsal Frank cruised into Crunchy's garage two hours late. He'd been getting later and later. He wore a brightly coloured shirt, jeans with holes all over them and a studded belt. His hair was greasy and slicked back.

"Hey dudes, what's going down?" asked Frank.

"You're late. Again," Crunchy snarled.

"Keep your shirt on, Crunchy. Had to sign some autographs, didn't I."

"All this attention has gone to your head," said Duck.

"It's a wonder you can fit it through the door," Bongo added.

Frank sneered at them. "You're all jealous."

"Jealous of what? Of you?" Crunchy, Duck and Bongo circled around him.

"Just because I play better guitar than you."

"Is that right? Then play me something." Crunchy had a funny look on his face.

"Easy."

Frank went for his guitar but Crunchy put his foot on the case. "No, not your guitar; play mine."

Frank blanched. "What?"

"That newspaper guy got me thinking about a few things."

"Thinking's a dangerous thing for you, Crunchy. Okay, I'll play your feeble excuse for a guitar."

Frank strapped on Crunchy's guitar and made a chord. It felt funny. He really had to press hard on the strings to make it play. His fingers were stiff and didn't move up the fretboard easily. He was playing like he did *before* he found his precious guitar. He stopped in disgust.

"As I thought." Crunchy looked very pleased with himself. "It's not you, it's that guitar."

Tears welled up in Frank's eyes. "I'm not going to hang around a bunch of wallies like you guys."

"Give it to me." Crunchy grabbed Frank's guitar. As his hands touched the strings, great blue sparks flew out of the guitar and up Crunchy's arm. The force blasted him across the room, and slammed him into the wall.

Everyone was shocked. Especially Crunchy. Frank grabbed his guitar and ran out.

Chapter 5

Dark Powers

Frank sat down on the sand and gazed at the waves. He hadn't gone surfing in ages. He looked at his guitar and sighed. What sort of guitar was it? And what about the old guy, and his knife that turned into a key then into a pin? How could he explain that? Only one way. Dark powers were at work, and Frank was caught up in them. He didn't know what to do.

• • •

When he got home a big, black car was parked outside his house. Mum and Dad were in the lounge room talking to a dark-haired man wearing a flashy business suit.

"Ah, here's our little prodigy." The suit-type stood and shook hands with Frank. His hand was icy-cold, and when he smiled he looked like an oily snake. Frank didn't like him at all.

"Mr Faust is a rock manager and he'd like to take over your career." Dad was glassy-eyed as he introduced the manager to Frank.

Frank was sure he'd seen the manager somewhere else before. It was something about his eyes: beady, but a bit cat-like.

"What's going on here, Mum?" asked Frank. Before she could answer, however, the manager butted in.

"How would you like to make a million dollars, son?" The manager grabbed Frank's shoulders.

Frank was stuck for words.

"That's right, Frank," drooled Dad. "We're going to be rich."

"But Dad..."

"Don't 'but' me son. It's up to you to make this family proud."

So that's how Frank found a manager. As for the guitar, Frank thought he had it under control. He was its master.

• • •

The same week Frank's manager organised interviews in *Woman's Day*, *Who*, *Rolling Stone*, and *Guitar* magazine. Frank was soon sick of answering the same stupid questions from inane reporters.

"How many guitars do you have?"

"One."

"How does it feel to be a rock-and-roll kid?"

"Good."

"What's your favourite ice cream? What's your favourite colour? What toothpaste do you use? What...what...what..."

Frank was no longer an everyday kid – he was a piece of merchandise. Something that could be sold. His manager was even talking about bringing out a "Frank" doll. You put batteries in and it would play guitar for you. Frank was beginning to feel a bit like a doll himself.

Then there was school. His schoolwork had gone right out the window. In fact he hadn't been to school for ages.

Dad wasn't worried. "No probs, mate, your career is all that counts now. With all the money you're making you can pay someone to go to school *for* you."

Mum didn't say anything.

• • •

Whenever the manager visited, Dad would start foaming at the mouth. Frank swore he could see dollar signs in Dad's eyes. "Of course the boy takes after me. I was a pretty mean hand on the guitar. Who knows – Australia today, tomorrow, the world. Or the next day!"

The manager just continued to smile his oily smile. Frank looked deeper into the manager's eyes until he remembered who he looked like. That was it. He had the same evil, cat-like eyes as the old man in the shop.

Frank didn't want any more of this fame business. All he wanted to do was play guitar with the Cool Cucumbers. But what could he do about it? Dad was in orbit scheming about his career, Mum was keeping her mouth shut, and the manager was smiling his oily smile. Worst of all, the guitar seemed to be getting stronger, and he was feeling weaker.

Chapter 6

Short Circuit

The bright lights of the studio shone right in Frank's eyes. He stood in front of the camera, squinting. He felt like a bug being examined under a microscope.

He was on "Midday with Kerri-Anne", with a band of seasoned performers behind him. Frank felt very young.

They started playing a bluesy number and Frank joined in. He thought of sadness and loneliness. It wasn't hard to do. A mournful sound came from his guitar. Frank could now understand the pain of anyone who was forced to be a slave.

After the show Frank's manager introduced Frank to a record company executive.

"That was beautiful playing, son."

Frank was tired. He just wanted to go home. "Yeah, right."

"You'll be the next silverchair."

"More like toiletseat," Frank feebly joked.

Frank's manager put a slimy arm around Frank's shoulders. "How would you like to go on tour, Frank?"

Frank felt weak at the knees. "A tour? But what about school?"

"We'll get you a private tutor." Frank's manager rubbed his hands. "Think of all those thousands of fans yelling your name. All wishing they were you."

Frank cringed. If only those fans knew. "I just want to be a normal kid again."

The manager gave Frank a deathly cold glare that shut him up. "That's enough of that talk. You are *not* normal. You are *special*. One of a kind."

The executive stared at Frank's guitar. "Talking of one of a kind, we should get rid of that monstrous piece of wood you play and find you a new guitar."

Frank's manager forced a laugh. "I've said the same thing but Frank just won't have it. He and that guitar are joined at the hip. He even sleeps with it."

The executive wasn't listening. "I can see it now." He grabbed the guitar from Frank. "You're on stage. You grab a small can of petrol and pour it on this beat-up beast. Then set fire to it. The band strikes up a rocking riff. Your brand-new, shiny guitar is then lowered from the roof. The stunt will send the fans crazy. It'll be fabulous!"

Frank could smell something. Petrol? The

executive screamed out in pain and dropped the guitar. He collapsed to the ground clutching at his left hand. It was burnt.

• • •

When the ambulance left, the manager glared at Frank. "What happened there?"

"I don't know." Frank shuffled nervously.

The manager opened Frank's case and examined the guitar. The petrol smell had gone. He stroked the guitar, deep in thought.

"Must have been a short circuit," he said finally.

Frank nodded. "Yeah, must have been." He went to close the case.

"Except it wasn't plugged in." The manager grabbed Frank and pointed at the guitar. "What *is* this thing?"

"It's evil."

"What are you talking about boy? How can a guitar be evil?"

"It's evil. No good. Possessed. Go and see

the old man, he'll explain everything."

"What old man? Who are you talking about?"

Frank tossed the manager the old man's business card. "You'll find out. Just don't sign any contracts." He ran out with his guitar.

Chapter 7

Bloodsucker

As Frank walked home carrying his guitar case he felt empty. Without planning it, Frank ended up outside Crunchy's house.

He could hear the band rehearsing. Crunchy was lead guitarist again. His playing had improved over time. He wasn't as good as Frank, of course. But at least Crunchy was doing it on his own. Frank wished he could just walk in and jam with the band. But he couldn't. He dragged himself home.

● ● ●

Frank picked up his dad's old acoustic guitar and started to play. Badly. He looked at himself in his mirror and shivered. He turned and gazed over at his electric guitar and for the first time he felt afraid. What he had seen in the mirror chilled him to the bone.

The guitar was feeding off him. Sucking the life from his body. Soon he'd be so thin that when he turned sideways he'd vanish. His hair was turning grey. His face was gaunt, and his eyes had sunk into their sockets. Crimson blotches were coming up all over his face. Worst of all, he could feel himself getting weaker. He was running out of time.

Frank spoke out loud. "Sorry, Dad. My life is more important than your ego. And as for that manager, he can bury his head."

Frank took the guitar out to the garage and locked it in a cupboard. He threw the key away. "That's the last time I play you, you bloodsucker." He went inside, picked up the old acoustic and started playing for real. It had the worst sound in the world, but it was *his* sound.

• • •

That night Frank felt tired, but elated. He cuddled up to Mum on the couch. Dad was counting bill posters.

"It's going to be great, Frank, this tour."

Frank's voice trembled. "I'm sick of playing that guitar. I'm never going to play it again."

Mum kissed Frank's head. "Good for you. That's the best news I've heard in a long time. I never liked that guitar. It wasn't the right colour." Mum gazed deep into Frank's eyes. Frank felt secure.

"You've got to be joking!" spluttered Dad, angrily. "What about all my plans for you? The fame, the glory, the money?"

"It's not fun any more, Dad."

"What's fun got to do with it? What about the contract I signed with the manager?"

Mum finally spoke. "Can't you see what's

happening to this boy? He's a wreck, both mentally and physically."

Dad steamed up. "It's just a virus. Look Frank, stop being such a prima donna. In the morning you get on with the plans for the tour."

"No, Dad."

"Don't 'no Dad' me, boy."

Frank had had enough. "Listen. It's over. Don't you get it? I'm finished being what you want me to be. I'm me. Not some younger version of you. If you really want what I've got, why don't you grab my guitar and go on tour yourself? Anyone can play it." He stormed out of the room.

• • •

Frank fell asleep quickly and dreamed that he was playing rhythm guitar with the Cool Cucumbers. Then he fell into a deeper sleep and his dreams became darker. He was back at the creepy second-hand shop. The old man was pointing to the contract, and Frank's drop of blood gleamed brightly in the flickering light.

"You can't get out of the contract. You must play the guitar. Forever."

"I won't. I'm not going to play it any more."

"Is that right? I think you'll find that the guitar has other ideas."

The guitar appeared out of the shadows. It sprang through the air and strapped itself onto Frank. Frank tried to resist but it was hopeless. The warmth he used to feel from the guitar had changed. Now it felt cold. It was as if the guitar was angry and was teaching him a lesson. He could feel the fretboard burrowing into his hand. He couldn't see where the guitar ended and his hand started. They were one.

Frank woke from the dream in a cold sweat. The guitar lay across his chest.

Chapter 8

Master and Servant

Frank found the second-hand shop and walked in. It smelled and looked exactly as it had before. The old man slunk out from the back room and smiled evilly at him.

"Ah, young guitar genius. I had a lovely chat with your manager yesterday."

"What did he say?"

"We've made a contract with you."

"How could you have made a contract with me if I wasn't there?"

41

"Ah, I have my ways. This is no ordinary contract, and you are going to have a blessed life."

"And a short one, if I listen to you."

"Think of all the money and fame you'll have."

"I'll be dead before it comes my way. Anyway, that doesn't matter. You can have your stinking guitar back."

"It's *your* guitar, remember?"

"Well, I don't want it any more."

"That's too bad. We made a contract."

"I want out of it."

The old man laughed and opened his mouth wide. His mouth was full of decayed teeth and his tongue was like a black, shrivelled worm.

"Do you think the guitar will give you up so easily? You two are halves of the one thing. Like Yin and Yang. Up and down. White and black. Master and servant."

Frank got very angry and shoved the guitar

at the old man. "Have it."

He turned and ran out of the shop. So he wasn't going to be a guitar hero any more. Big deal. He just felt relieved that he was rid of it. At least he wasn't going to live a lie...

Suddenly, Frank doubled over in pain. He felt weak, and crampy pains shot through his stomach. His heart started to beat oddly, like a gigantic hand was squeezing it. *It was the guitar.*

He staggered back to the shop, and the old man stood grinning in the doorway, waiting for him. "I think you forgot this," he cackled.

Frank took the guitar and weakly turned for home.

• • •

Frank collapsed onto his bed and tossed the guitar across the room. As it hit the ground an intense pain shot up his back. Frank screamed. The guitar and he were one. What was he going to do? He couldn't destroy the guitar. He couldn't get rid of it. He was stuck with it.

Through the pain, a sudden thought flashed into his head. The guitar and he were one. *One*. That was it. But was he up to it? Was he brave enough to go through with it?

Chapter 9

Feedback!

Frank stood in his garage and took the cover off his dad's old amp. It was really beat-up looking. It had tinny looking knobs. Wire hanging out the back. Black tape holding it together. It was a real home-made job.

Frank turned on the amp and it hissed and burped into life. A few sparks shot out the back. He touched the volume knob and felt an electrical thrill go through his hand. The amp had definite shock value. Using a stick, Frank moved the volume knob as far up as it could go. A loud buzz came out of the speaker.

Frank strapped on his guitar and, using his dad's old guitar lead, plugged it into the amp. The amp screeched loudly, like an alley-cat spitting and spraying. He felt the guitar buck in his hand, and a searing pain shot though his fingertips and up to his head.

"Okay, we're joined at the hip. I feel what you feel. Well, two can play at that game."

Frank tightened the machine heads holding the strings as tightly as he could. Every turn of the screws could be felt in Frank's head. He twisted the switches on the guitar until they snapped, and felt one of his teeth crack in the back of his mouth.

"Now, let's get down to some seriously bad playing."

Frank was still for a moment, as he tried to imagine how the worst guitarist in the world – himself! – would play the guitar if it wasn't bewitched. In short, he imagined a rank beginner. Frank placed his fingers on the strings and felt an icy hold take over them. But he fought against it with all his might. Then he started playing. Badly. *Really* badly.

The guitar squealed out a totally out-of-key, off-tempo, wrong-tone solo that would make the dead turn in their graves. It and Frank wrestled with each other. The guitar squeezed Frank's hand tighter and tighter. Frank felt the pain but continued playing – *his* way.

Frank bent the strings all the way off the fretboard. The top three guitar strings snapped off with a loud, twanging noise. It sounded like an animal yelping in pain.

"Sucked in, guitar."

Frank picked up the intensity. He played notes that shouldn't be played together. The noise sounded like a semi-trailer pile-up. Frank's ears were ringing; even bleeding. His body burned red hot. Oily, hot sweat oozed out of his pores. The shriek of the amp pulsated painfully through every cell in his body. But he could feel the guitar's power ebbing.

Then Frank pulled out his big gun.

"Try this on for size." Frank turned the guitar to face his dad's amp. Blue smoke was pouring out of the back of the amp, and it screeched and belched in protest at Frank's hideous playing. He shoved the guitar right up against the amp and made heavy-metal feedback noises.

The guitar's neck bent away from the amp but Frank held it firm. There was an almighty howling note – and the neck split in two. The guitar became quiet as the amp blew up in a mass of smoke and sparks. Frank collapsed to the ground, exhausted but victorious.

Suddenly the old man appeared out of thin air. "What are you doing to my beautiful guitar?" he screamed.

"Whose guitar? It's mine, remember. I can

do what I like with it." Frank laughed.

"I'll take it back."

Frank had won, but he wanted to make the victory complete. "How much?" he asked.

"What?" The old man seemed to grow bigger and uglier. He moved towards Frank and stared into his face. "Don't toy with me, boy."

Frank imagined the guitar going up in flames. The charred remnants of the guitar body buckled and twisted on the garage floor, and the old man flinched in pain.

"Okay, okay. You win." The old man pulled out a wad of hundred dollar notes and flung them at Frank. "There you are." He pulled the contract from his ragged sleeve and tore it up. Then he picked up the pieces of the guitar and disappeared.

Frank collapsed to the ground. The connection between him and the guitar was finally broken. His body ached intensely, but he smiled.

Chapter 10

Back to Earth

When Frank's dad finally came down to earth, he came down with a crash. He knew he'd acted badly. He stood sheepishly in front of Frank.

"I'm sorry, mate, I don't know what came over me. I'm so ashamed of what I put you through. Can you ever forgive me?"

"That's okay, Dad."

Mum linked arms with Frank and Dad. She smiled widely and then nodded at Frank. Frank handed Dad back his old guitar. "I think you should have this back," said Frank, smiling. "It's been ages since I played my guitar."

Frank picked up the brand-new guitar and amp he'd bought with the old man's money. "I'll see you later."

Dad was already strumming his old guitar. "Maybe when you come home we can have a jam."

"I'd like that. Oh, I'm sorry about your amp." Frank ducked out of the door quickly.

"What about my amp?"

Mum interrupted. "Play me a love song."

• • •

The following week, Frank walked past the old man's shop. It was black and charred, and the old man was nowhere to be seen. Everything inside was burnt beyond recognition. It was said that an incense burner had toppled over; that it was the biggest fire the fire brigade had ever seen.

The manager had also disappeared off the face of the earth. The only thing the police found at his house when investigating his disappearance was a crumpled, smeared piece of paper, dotted with pin-pricks of blood.

• • •

The Cool Cucumbers hadn't been as successful after Frank left. If their playing didn't improve, there was a chance that they'd lose the disco gig. Crunchy tried to sing and play at the same time but he just couldn't get it right. As he mucked-up their third practice song, Duck sniggered.

"You aren't a bad guitar player, Crunchy, but you can't sing to save your life. We need a singer."

As if on cue, Frank appeared in the doorway. Crunchy took one look at him and grinned. "You'll do."

"What if I can't sing?"

"Anything's better than my pitiful singing. And don't you know that girls love rhythm-guitarist-singers?"

"What if I don't want to re-join the band?"

Crunchy handed the microphone to Frank. The band started playing. In time and in key. Frank joined in, and the band came alive.

During his guitar solo, Crunchy whispered into Frank's ear. "By the way, my shoes are just over there. So after rehearsal's over, get your tongue out and start licking."

About the Author

Brian McGinn is an Intensive Care Unit nurse. He lives near Wollongong with his wife, son and daughter.

Brian has written several plays, and a series for ABC Radio called "Alien Evangelist". *Hell-ectric Guitar* is his first novel.

Bargains from Outer Space
by Heather Hammonds

Rod and Sean get more than they bargain for when they flick through the channels on the new TV. Who, or what, are the strange creatures selling fantastic gadgets? And do they really deliver? Find out what happens when Rod and Sean go on a shopping spree that is out-of-this-world!

Birthday Surprise
by Margaret Pearce

Freckles, Frazzle and James think they'll surprise their mother on her birthday with a plant they have grown themselves. The birthday plant however, shows a sinister appetite for food – and worse!

The Twins in the Trunk

by Susan Green

When Katie finds an old trunk in the cellar under her house, she thinks she's found bushranger's treasure. What she has found is ghost trouble – and double trouble at that! Katie and Angus soon find that some things are better left unopened...

Monopillar

by Alan Horsfield

A weird alien mystery set in and around Sydney's Powerhouse Museum. Who are the mysterious scientists, and why are they carrying bags of bones around? And why is the Monorail looking so strange?

BlitzIt is here! Once you've read one
BlitzIt book, you'll want to read them all.

Mystery ... adventure ... alien visitors ...
weird science ... spooky happenings ...
BlitzIt has something for everyone!

Expiry Date

by Raewyn Caisley

Quentin and Andrew think it's pretty funny to
tease Richard Corelli. Things go terribly wrong
however, and Andrew finds himself haunted by
a mysterious stranger. Could Andrew be
approaching his "expiry date"?